"Good-bye, Grandma."

"Good-bye, Francie," said Grandma. "You both take care.
It's wet out there and such a long way home."

"We will, won't we, Mommy?" replied Francie.

"Of course we will," said Mom.

Their little red car seemed to muster all of its courage
as it waited outside, ready for the road.

For Cormac and Dervla

Rain is grace; rain is the sky condescending to the earth; without rain, there would be no life.
John Updike

Home in the Rain

BOB GRAHAM

CANDLEWICK PRESS

Didn't it rain!

It hit the highway, bucketing down on Francie and her mom
and her baby sister on their way home from Grandma's.

It rained on endless lines of cars and buses, oil tankers and
trucks, the windshield wipers in despair. *Shoo-shoo-shoo!*

But the rain was going nowhere.
Except down.
Francie, Mom, and Baby Sister,
a long way from home.

A big rig passed on a long-haul trip,
headed for Heaven knows where!
It rocked them in road spray and
washed them up into the picnic area.

Above the highway it rained on the hill,
and a baby rabbit dived for cover.

It rained on a field mouse, wet and confused
in the blackberries—and lucky, too . . .

because three hundred
feet up, a kestrel had lost
sight of its prey!

It rained on the canal,
turning the water white,
and it rained on the fishermen,
wet as the fish below.

Young Marcus, water
running down his neck,
his fingers smelling of bait,
wished he were
somewhere else . . .

while the water ran off the
backs of ducks.

The rain soaked two men on the Western Highway interchange.
They argued while steam rose from their hot engines.

And not looking where it was going, the countryside ran straight into the edge of the highway, bringing with it the faint smell of farmyards.

Francie, Mom, and Baby Sister,
such a long way from home.

Inside Francie's car the fog
moved in. She wrote her name
in her breath on the side window.

She wrote her mom's name
with her finger squeaking on the glass.

And then her dad's name.
Her dad working far out to sea,
gone three weeks now.
She wrote it clear across
the front window.

"My little sister.
 What will her name be, Mommy?"
"Well, she's not quite with us yet," said Mom.
"But when will she have a name, Mommy?" said Francie.
"Soon," said Mom. "Sometime soon."

Francie saw a whole back window just waiting for a name . . .

a window just waiting for Francie's wet finger.

"Could it be Alice, maybe? Or Isabel . . . Emma . . . or, um, Zoe?"

"Well, they're nice, Francie," said Mom, "but there's a name somewhere out there that will fit her just right."

They ate the picnic Grandma had packed.
Plum jam sandwiches and hard-boiled eggs
with a little sprinkle of salt.
They shared the two stale toffees found
under old parking tickets in the door.

"When is Daddy coming home?" said Francie.
"Soon," replied Mom. "Sometime soon."
"Like the new baby, then," said Francie,
and felt a small movement against her ear.
"Well . . . yes," said Mom, brushing crumbs
from her knees. "Like the new baby."

Then the radio played.
"This is 3LFM, your spot on the radio.
It's wet on the road. So you take care, folks."

Francie and her mom
and her baby sister pulled
back out into the traffic.

Far off down the road they found a service station.
Hail hit the roof, and oil on the puddles made rainbows
around Francie's toes.

What was about
to happen would
not be noticed
by anyone.

Not by Sam Miller
feeding his dog fried
chicken legs.

Nor by Kate Calder losing her Sour Fruity Fizzes
from a hole in her pocket.

Not even by a seagull
who was eating them.

Perhaps it was something unremarkable,
not to be seen by strangers passing in the rain.
For it was just a mom lost in thought
and a small girl dancing.

"Francie, come here,"
said Mom.

"Grace! Your new sister—
we'll call her Grace!"
And Mom hugged Francie as best
she could with Francie's sister,
Grace, in between.

The three of them.

They staggered and toppled
a bit, did a slow and awkward
little dance of their own.
Until Francie's feet found
the ground again.

Francie had a feeling.
She knew right here—with the smell of gasoline
and her feet all wet on the pavement in the rain—
that she would remember this moment forever!
"Wait until Daddy hears," said Francie.
"Daddy will love that," replied Mom.

And way back down the highway, Francie's grandma sipped tea, rabbits and field mice were deep in their burrows, young Marcus headed home for a hot bath, and somewhere, kestrel chicks went without dinner.

Then the sun covered the countryside—far off and away
from Grandma's place to home and out across the sea.
Their little car, now full of courage, bumped off down the
road, the windows rolled down and wind rushing through.

One window was still fogged up.
It had Francie's fading breath
and *GRACE* still faintly showing.